meRMaiDs ROCK

The Ice Giant

To Becky Hodgkins, one of my biggest fans!—L.C.

To all the people helping to build a better world—M.O.

tiger tales

5 River Road, Suite 128, Wilton, CT 06897
Published in the United States 2021
Originally published in Great Britain 2020
by the Little Tiger Group
Text copyright © 2020 Linda Chapman
Illustrations copyright © 2020 Mirelle Ortega
ISBN-13: 978-1-6643-4001-5
ISBN-10: 1-6643-4001-7
Printed in the USA
STP/4800/0426/0821
2 4 6 8 10 9 7 5 3 1

www.tigertalesbooks.com

MERMAIDS ROCK

The Ice Giant

by Linda Chapman
Illustrated by Mirelle Ortega

tiger tales

Contents

Welcome to Mermaids Rock!

Marina &
Sammy

Kai & Tommy

Naya &
Octavia

Coralie & Dash

Luna &
Melly

Chapter One
Turtle Tricks

"Roll over, Tommy!" Kai said hopefully.

Tommy, Kai's hawksbill sea turtle, tipped his head to one side, his dark eyes puzzled.

"Look, watch me, Tommy. When I say roll over, you do this." Kai flicked the end of his orange-red tail and rolled over and over in the warm turquoise water. "Now you try. Roll over and keep going until I say stop. Go on!"

Tommy turned onto his back, pulled his head inside his gold-and-brown shell, and stuck his stubby flippers straight up.

"No! That's playing dead," Kai said in frustration. He pushed a hand through his thick dark hair. He'd been trying to teach Tommy to roll over for an hour now. The Spring Fair was only a week away, and this year, there was going to be a contest for the most talented pet. Kai really wanted to enter Tommy, so he was trying to teach him some tricks.

Just then, a mergirl with a silvery-green tail came over. She had a little gold-and-yellow seahorse with her. Its tail was curled around a lock of her thick brown hair. "Hi, Kai. How's it going?" she asked as Tommy righted himself and swam up to say hello. He nuzzled her with his armored head.

"It's not going well at all, Marina," admitted Kai as Marina gently scratched under Tommy's chin. Kai and Marina had been friends ever since Marina had moved to Mermaids Rock with her father a few months ago. "Tommy just doesn't seem to want to learn any tricks. So far, I've tried teaching him to shake flippers, play dead, and roll over, but he's not doing any of them when I ask, even though I know he can do them."

Kai suddenly realized that, although Marina was usually chatty and smiley, today she looked upset. "Are you okay?" he asked.

Marina shook her head. "No. Not really. It's my dad. He—"

She was interrupted by a sneering laugh. "Are you seriously trying to teach that brainless turtle tricks, Kai Stormchaser? I don't know why you're bothering. You have no chance in the pet talent contest!"

Kai swung around. Glenda Seaglass, a mergirl with long, blond hair, was watching them with her two friends, Jazeela and Racquel. Kai liked almost everyone who lived in the reef, but not Glenda—she was as mean as a viperfish.

"Tommy is not brainless!" Marina protested.

"No, he's very clever," said Kai loyally.

"Oh, really?" said Glenda. "Let's see then."
She swam over to the turtle. "Roll over! Go
on!" she commanded.

Tommy thought for a moment and then
offered her a flipper.

Glenda and her friends snickered. "Oh, yes,
very clever," said Glenda. "I don't think so!"

"He has about as much brain as a sea jelly,"
sneered Racquel.

"Just like Kai!" added Glenda.

The three mergirls squealed
with unkind laughter.

"Oh, go away," Marina said angrily as Kai hugged Tommy, hoping his feelings weren't hurt. "It's not like you're taking part in the talented-pet competition, Glenda. You don't even have one!"

"Oh, I don't?" Glenda smirked. "Shows how much you know, Marina Silverfin. My father's getting me a pet—a really *fin-tastic* one—so all of you in your little Save the Sea Creatures Club had better watch out. My new pet is going to win, and no one else will have a chance. Come on," she said to Jazeela and Racquel. "Let's leave these two to their terrible turtle training."

They giggled and swam off.

"Ignore them," Marina said to Tommy. "You're wonderful."

Kai nodded. "They're the brainless ones." He scratched Tommy's head, and the turtle waggled a back flipper in delight.

"I feel really sorry for whatever poor pet

Glenda gets," said Marina.

"I don't understand how she thinks she might win," said Kai, puzzled. "Even if she gets a new pet, she won't have time to train it before the contest. There's only a week to go."

"You'll have to make sure you beat her," Marina said firmly.

"Or you and Sammy could," said Kai. "You are entering the contest, aren't you?"

Sammy, Marina's little seahorse, looked at Marina. She bit her lip. "We're … um … we're not going to be able to enter because we won't be here."

Kai looked at her in surprise. What did she mean? "Why? Where will you be?"

"My dad wants to go to the Arctic to do some research on Atlantic walruses," Marina said sadly.

Kai's heart sank. Marina's dad, a merman named Tarak, was a marine scientist, and he had to travel a lot with his work.

"There are fewer and fewer walruses every year," Marina continued, "and he wants to find out why. We're leaving Mermaids Rock in the next few days so that he can do his research before the spring thaw starts in the Arctic. That means I won't be here for the fair." Marina swallowed. "Oh, Kai, I know it'll be amazing to go to the Arctic, but I love it here in the reef at Mermaids Rock. I don't want to leave school or you and Luna, Naya, and Coralie. We've had so much fun together since I moved here—having adventures and being in the Save the Sea Creatures Club." She looked really upset.

"How long will you be away?" Kai asked, feeling awful for her.

"I'm not sure, but maybe a few months," Marina said gloomily.

"A few months!" echoed Kai. "That's forever!"

Marina nodded and turned to pet Sammy. Kai could tell she was trying to hide how unhappy she was.

"No!" he declared suddenly, and Marina looked up in surprise. "We won't let this happen! You're not going, Marina Silverfin. We're not going to let you!"

A reluctant smile tugged at Marina's lips. "And how do you plan on stopping my dad, Kai?"

"I don't know. We could trap him in a giant clam or a vase sponge...." Kai's thoughts raced wildly. "Or we'll find something so amazing here in the reef that he has to stay and study that instead...."

Tommy suddenly swam over to Marina, took her hand gently in his mouth, and tugged her toward the entrance of the coral cave where Kai lived with his mom.

"What are you doing, Tommy?" Marina asked in astonishment.

Kai looked at his turtle closely. Whatever Glenda and her gaggle of mean friends might say, he knew Tommy was really intelligent.

Tommy stopped by the cave entrance and looked at Kai. He wrinkled his knobbly forehead as if to say, "Well?"

"What is it, Tommy?" asked Kai.

In reply, Tommy swam around Marina and pushed her into the cave.

"Kai! Control your turtle! He's gone crazy!" she giggled, scrambling away from him.

"No! I get it!" exclaimed Kai suddenly. "Tommy's trying to tell us he thinks you should stay here with me and Mom. We have a big cave—you and Sammy could easily fit in, too. Your dad can go off researching in the Arctic, and you can stay here with us."

"Oh, bubbles! Do you think your mom would agree?" Marina gasped.

"Only one way to find out," said Kai. "She's on duty by the whirlpool. Last one there is a stinky hagfish!"

Kai and Marina charged across the reef. They whooshed through shoals of tiny orange-and-black fish, swerved around gliding turtles and slow-moving manatees, and raced past clumps of brightly colored sea sponges until they found Indra, Kai's mom, patrolling near the entrance of Mermaids Rock. She was one of the merguards who protected the merpeople's beautiful coral reef from dangerous predators, like reef sharks and killer whales.

The guards had also recently started using spells to keep the reef hidden from human eyes. It was right in the middle of the Indian Ocean, and humans never used to come near it. However, recently, they had started exploring the more remote areas of the world's oceans, and a few boats had been spotted. The guards had cast cloaking spells with their tridents so that if a boat ever came close to the reef, the humans would only see an empty stretch of ocean, and they would feel a strong urge to sail in the opposite direction.

Kai's mom was swimming beside a huge rock that jutted up from the seabed. It was shaped like a mermaid's tail, and a magic whirlpool swirled around at its base. The whirlpool could transport the merpeople to any sea or ocean in the world. They used it to try to keep the oceans of the world clean and to protect the marine creatures who lived in all those different environments.

"Mom! Mom!" Kai shouted. "Can Marina come and live with us while her dad goes away?"

Kai's mom lowered her three-pronged trident and listened carefully as the whole story came pouring out of the two merchildren.

She smiled as they finished. "Of course, you and Sammy are welcome to stay with us, Marina—if your dad is happy with the idea."

"Oh, thank you!" Marina gasped.

"What's going on here?" demanded a stern voice. They turned and saw a dark-haired merman with a pointy beard swimming toward them. It was Razeem Seaglass, the Chief of the Guards. He was Glenda's father, and like Glenda, he was very bossy.

"Nothing, Chief Razeem," said Kai's mom, quickly raising her trident again. "Kai and Marina just stopped by to ask me something."

"They should know better than to disturb you at work," Chief Razeem replied disapprovingly. He shooed at them with his hands. "Go on now. Move along, children!" He turned to Kai's mom. "I need you to come with me. There are some porpoises ready to be assessed."

Kai's mom nodded. The merguards used specially selected porpoises for search-and-rescue work, and these animals were highly intelligent and well trained.

"I'll see you both later when I finish work," said Kai's mom as she swam off with Chief Razeem. "Go and talk to your dad, Marina, and tell him that I said you're very welcome to stay with us."

"Thank you!" called Marina. She flicked her tail eagerly. "Come on, Kai! Let's go!"

Chapter Two
Fire
Potion

On the way back to Marina's cave, Kai spotted the other members of the Save the Sea Creatures Club—Naya, Coralie, and Coralie's younger cousin, Luna. Coralie and Naya were racing in and out of a row of giant purple-and-pink sea sponges with their pets—Dash the dolphin and Octavia the octopus. Luna and her gentle manatee, Melly, were judging the races, although it wasn't a hard job—Coralie and Dash were super speedy and won every time!

"Hi there!" Coralie called, waving at Kai and Marina, her dark-red hair swirling around her shoulders as she stopped abruptly. "Where have you two been?"

"We stopped by your caves to see if you wanted to come and play, but you weren't there," Naya added.

Kai and Marina explained what had been happening.

"So you're really going to stay at Kai's and not go to the Arctic?" said Luna hopefully, slipping her hand into Marina's.

"If Dad says yes. We're going to ask him now—he should be home."

"He didn't answer when we came over earlier," Naya pointed out.

"Oh, you know what he's like," said Marina, rolling her eyes. "He was probably busy with work and didn't even hear!"

Kai grinned. Marina's dad often got so absorbed in what he was doing that he didn't notice anything going on around him. Sometimes, he would even forget to eat or sleep!

"He's going to study walruses?" said Coralie enviously. "Wow! Just think of the incredible things he'll see in the Arctic!"

"He might see polar bears and their cubs," said Luna, her eyes shining. She loved all animals and had an amazing knack for being able to instantly make friends with any of them.

"There will be seals, too," said Naya. "And birds like Arctic terns. Not to mention the different ice formations. I'd love to see glaciers calving!"

Kai was puzzled. "Calving? Is a glacier a type of whale?"

Naya giggled. "No, silly! A glacier is an enormous frozen river that edges its way across land until it reaches the sea. Calving is when the ice at the end of the glacier separates and falls off into the water. That's how icebergs are made. They come in different shapes and sizes, and the ice in them shifts and changes as they thaw and refreeze."

"You know so much, Naya!" Luna said, impressed.

"She does, but I bet she doesn't know what one iceberg says to another when they play hide-and-seek," said Coralie, her eyes sparkling.

Naya raised her eyebrows. "What does it say?"

Coralie giggled. "I thaw you!"

They groaned. Coralie's jokes were the worst!

Naya shook her head, making the glass beads at the end of her long braids clink together. She turned to Marina. "Do you think your dad will let us visit him while he's in the Arctic? I bet the Save the Sea Creatures Club could have a *foam-tastic* adventure there!"

"That would be great! But first I need to make sure that he'll let me stay in Mermaids Rock," said Marina. "Let's find him and ask!"

At Mermaids Rock, the merpeople lived in caves in the coral reef. Marina and her dad's cave was near Kai's. It had a large central living space with a huge pot of magical mermaid fire in the middle. The uneven coral walls formed natural shelves, and they were filled with interesting items that Marina and her dad had collected on their travels—a narwhal's horn, a giant sea star from Australia, a string of beautiful pearls, and a bunch of different shells and stones. The walls were newly covered with charts written on sea parchment showing climate and weather conditions around the world, as well as strings of cowrie shells threaded onto ribbon seaweed that Marina had made. There were three smaller caves leading off of the main space—two bedrooms and a study.

Marina's dad was in the study, packing test tubes and bottles of different colored chemicals into a case. He looked surprised to see them all. "Hello!"

Marina quickly told him about Kai's mom's offer. "You know I love coming with you to do research, Dad, but I also love it here at Mermaids Rock. I really want to keep going to school and stay with my friends. But only if you think you'll be able to manage without me." Marina gave her dad a slightly worried look.

To Kai's delight, Marina's dad smiled and kissed Marina on the head. "Of course I'll manage. I'll miss you, but if you want to stay, and Kai's mom is happy to have you, then that's fine by me. In fact, it may be for the best. This trip could be dangerous."

Marina frowned. "What do you mean? I thought you said you were going to research walruses—they're usually gentle, aren't they?"

Her dad nodded. "They're one of nature's gentle giants, but sometimes they stampede, and you really don't want to be in the way when a hundred walruses are charging. There are also other dangers in the Arctic at this time of year. The polar bears will be hungry and out hunting on the sea ice."

"Sea ice? I didn't think the sea ever froze," said Luna.

"Only in places like the Arctic," said Marina's dad. "It freezes in the fall and makes a thick platform that polar bears use for hunting and

22

walruses for resting on. Then in the spring, as it gets warmer, the sea ice starts to break up and melts away. When that happens, a lot of the animals, like polar bears, travel north to where it's colder. I need to go now because once the ice starts to melt, the waters will be too dangerous to swim in. There will be floating ice sheets and icebergs, not to mention beluga and bowhead whales migrating. Human boats are also more likely to arrive to fish and sightsee as the ice breaks up."

"It does sound dangerous.... Are you sure you should go?" Marina asked her dad, sounding concerned.

"I must," he said. "The number of Atlantic walruses is falling every year, and I want to try to find out why."

"What about all of the ice? Won't you get cold?" asked Coralie.

"Ah! Thankfully, I have my latest invention," said Marina's dad. He took a little bottle off a shelf. It had red powder in the bottom. "Look at this!"

"What is it?" said Kai curiously. The tiny bottle didn't look like it could keep anyone warm.

"It's a special powder made from deep-sea algae, minerals, dried kelp, and a pinch of magical mermaid powder," said Marina's dad, his eyes gleaming enthusiastically. "When I mix the powder in this bottle with salt water, it causes an exothermic reaction."

"That's a chemical reaction that gives off heat, isn't it?" Naya said as the rest of them looked at one another blankly.

Marina's dad nodded. "Correct, Naya. If I drink a bottle of this, it will keep me warm from the inside out for 24 hours. As long as I drink one bottle every day, then I'll be fine. I call it Fire Potion."

"Wow, that's amazing!" Naya enthused. "Oh, I so want to be a scientist like you when I'm older!"

Marina's dad smiled. "I'm sure you will be."

Marina frowned. "Dad, I'm going to be really worried about you."

"You mustn't be. I'll be all right," he reassured her. "I'll be back before you know it. Now, I really need to finish packing," he said, turning back to his desk. "I'm heading out in two days."

"We'll leave you to it," said Marina, and they went into the living space.

"Your dad will be okay," said Kai, seeing Marina's worried face. "He's traveled all over the ocean."

"Yes, he'll be fine," Naya agreed.

Marina nodded. "I know. I'm just worried that he'll get so absorbed in his work that he'll forget to eat or go to bed without me to remind him." She frowned. "I need to take my mind off of it. Why don't we do more of those races you were playing? They looked fun!"

Back in the reef, they continued racing, but Marina had the idea of adding an obstacle course. As well as weaving between the sea sponges, they had to swim through a tunnel of coral, dodge around a giant clam three times, and turn two somersaults before racing to the finish line. Coralie and Dash were the fastest, but Kai and Tommy were very quick at turning, and Marina and Sammy were the best at somersaulting. Naya dropped out to judge with Luna: they definitely needed two pairs of eyes to decide who was first across the finish line each time. Eventually, they heard Luna's mom calling to them.

"Hi, Aunt Erin," said Coralie as the older mermaid spotted them and swam over. Coralie gave her aunt a hug. "How's the sanctuary? Did you get any interesting animals in today?"

Luna's mom worked at the marine animal sanctuary, where sick or hurt sea creatures were nursed back to health. The Save the Sea Creatures Club sometimes found injured creatures out in the reef and took them to her.

Aunt Erin ran a hand through her long, red hair. She looked tired but happy. "It's been a busy day, but a good one. I've successfully stitched up a manta ray who had an injured wing, operated on a turtle who'd eaten a plastic straw, and I've been taking care of the orphaned baby manatee."

"How's he doing?" Kai asked. They'd seen the cute baby manatee when they'd last visited the sanctuary. He had been found by himself and was too young to survive on his own, so Aunt Erin was hand-rearing him.

Aunt Erin's eyes glowed. "Really well. I'm sure he's going to be fine, and when he's a little older, I'll be able to find him a good home."

Most of the time, the creatures that came

into the sanctuary could be helped and returned to the wild, but those that couldn't—usually the ones who had been orphaned when they were babies—ended up becoming pets, like Tommy and the others.

"Are you going to take him to the Spring Fair, Aunt Erin?" Coralie asked.

"I don't think so. It'll be a little too busy for him," said Aunt Erin. "He's still very little."

"Ooh, now that I'm going to be staying here, I'll be able to enter Sammy in the pet talent contest after all!" Marina realized.

Sammy bobbed up and down happily.

"What will you and Sammy do?" asked Kai curiously.

"He's pretty good at fetching things, so maybe we can show off that talent," said Marina. "Sammy, can you go and get me a white pebble?" she said, pointing to the sea floor. Sammy drifted down, curled his tail around a little white pebble, lifted it carefully, and bobbed back.

"Great job!" Marina praised.

Aunt Erin smiled. "He's such a cutie, Marina."

Marina beamed. "Thank you!"

"I'm sure you'll do very well in the pet competition, Sammy," Aunt Erin said to the seahorse. "You'll show everyone that you don't have to be big to be talented, won't you?" He swam over to her and kissed her cheek with his tiny snout. She grinned. "That tickles!"

Kai remembered what Glenda had said earlier about getting a new pet. Had it come from the sanctuary? "Have you given any animals to Glenda Seaglass recently, Aunt Erin?"

"Glenda?" Aunt Erin echoed. "No, she never comes into the sanctuary." She waved good-bye to them as she and Luna left.

Marina looked at Kai. "Where is Glenda getting her amazing new pet from, then?"

"What new pet?" asked Coralie.

Kai and Marina told Coralie and Naya what Glenda had said.

Coralie groaned. "I hope she doesn't enter and win with this *fin-tabulous* new pet of hers. She's so annoying!"

"As irritating as a sting from a giant sea jelly," agreed Marina.

"So, what do you think this new pet is? And what is she going to train it to do?" said Naya.

Kai frowned. "I guess we'll just have to wait and see."

Chapter Three
Off to the Arctic

The next two days flew by. Marina packed up her things and moved them into Kai and Indra's cave. There was a spare bed where she and Sammy could sleep. Luckily, it was spring break, so there was plenty of time to get everything figured out. Marina helped her dad finish packing up his research gear, but Kai could tell that she was still worried about the trip, even though she was putting on a brave face.

"I just wish there was a way Dad could let me know he was all right," Marina said to Kai on the morning her dad was due to leave. They were sitting outside Kai's cave while Sammy practiced fetching pebbles and Tommy nosed around the crevices in the coral, searching for shrimp and krill to eat.

Kai hated seeing any of his friends unhappy. He searched his mind for a solution. "Maybe he could write you letters and send them through the whirlpool."

Marina shook her head. "He'd find having to write letters to be too much of a distraction from his work."

Kai looked at the little pile of pebbles Sammy had collected. "How about asking him to drop a stone into the whirlpool every day? That wouldn't be too much of a distraction. He could throw a white stone in if everything is okay and a red stone if he's in trouble and needs help."

Marina's eyes widened. "That's a really good idea. Thanks, Kai!"

When it was time for Marina's dad to leave, they all swam with him to the whirlpool.

"Now, don't worry about Marina," Kai's mom said to Marina's dad. "I'll take good care of her."

"I know you will," said Marina's dad. "Thank you."

Marina hugged him. "Promise me you'll throw a stone into the whirlpool every day?"

She had told her dad about Kai's idea, and

he'd agreed it was a clever way of staying in touch. She'd given him a bag full of the white stones Sammy had collected, along with a couple of red ones—although she hoped he wasn't going to need those! She'd drawn an M on each stone so she would know that the stones that came through the whirlpool every day were definitely from him.

"I won't miss a day," he said. "I promise. Don't worry about me, sweetheart. I'll be fine."

Marina hoped he was right. "And you promise you'll remember to drink your Fire Potion?"

"Yes, I will. The bottles are safe in here," said her dad, patting the large backpack on his back.

"I made something to help keep you warm, too," said Naya shyly. She opened her bag. "I thought your Fire Potion idea was amazing, so I adapted it and made these." She pulled out a clear box of tiger-striped clamshells. They were cream with pale pink and peach stripes, each about the size of a hand.

Marina's dad took the bag curiously. "How do they work?"

"In each shell, there's a bag containing a mix of algae, dried kelp, minerals, and mermaid powder. If you open the shell and add seawater to the mixture, an exothermic reaction happens, like with your Fire Potion. When you shut the shell, the heat is trapped inside, and it becomes a hand warmer." Naya blushed as Marina's dad stared at her. "I hope you don't mind my copying your idea."

"Mind? Of course not! This is a wonderful invention, Naya." Marina's dad beamed at her. "Great job, and thank you very much. I'm sure they'll be really useful."

"They'll come in —" Coralie giggled— "handy. Get it? A hand warmer—handy?"

The others flicked their tails at her.

"And on that note, I'll be off," said Marina's

dad. He pulled Marina in close for one last hug and then turned to the whirlpool. "Take me to the Arctic—to the sea north of Baffin Bay!" he declared.

The water started to churn faster and faster, turning into frothy white foam.

"Good-bye!" shouted Marina's dad as he dove in. The water swirled even faster, and then after a few seconds, it began to slow down.

"He's gone," Marina said softly.

"He'll be back soon," said Kai's mom, squeezing her arm. "And just think of the stories he'll have to tell you."

Sammy kissed Marina's nose, and Kai saw her force a smile. "Let's do something fun," he said quickly, wanting to cheer her up. "I vote we play stuck-in-the-silt. Tommy and I will be It!"

"See you later!" Kai's mom called.

They sped off, with Kai and Tommy chasing after them. Whenever anyone was caught, they had to stay still in the water, pretending they were stuck in sticky silt, and hold their arms or flippers out until someone else swam under them and then they could set off again. Tommy was super speedy, zipping through the water and turning sharply. Only Dash, Coralie, and Octavia managed to get away from him. Poor Melly, who could rarely be bothered to swim quickly, got caught over and over again.

"Let's do something else!" begged Luna after a while. "How about hide-and-seek?"

"Or sardines!" said Marina. "One person and their pet hide, and when someone finds them, they have to hide with them. You can go as far as the meadow where the sea dragons hatched, but no farther. okay?"

"Okay!" the friends chorused.

"Who's going to hide first?" said Kai.

"You and Tommy," Coralie said. "Tommy is too good at finding people." Turtles had a very keen sense of smell underwater, and Tommy was great at sniffing out people. Kai loved being on a team with him whenever they played hide-and-seek!

"You count to a hundred!" Kai said. While the others covered their eyes and started to count, he grabbed Tommy's shell, and they shot off through the coral. There were so many places to hide—inside caves, in a gigantic old shell, behind a branching sea fan....

In the end, they darted into a clump of tall, cylindrical sea sponges and hid in the center, pulling some seaweed over them for even better coverage.

"There's room for the others to hide with us here—if they can find us!" whispered Kai as he crouched beside Tommy. "But we need to stay still and quiet." Tommy blinked his little dark eyes at Kai, and his wrinkled mouth turned up into a smile. He was good at staying still and quiet when he wanted to.

"You're good at so many things," Kai whispered, scratching his head. "Just not the tricks I'm trying to teach you."

Marina and Sammy were the first to find them, and then Naya and Octavia. Luna and Melly were next. They crouched together, trying not to giggle as they heard Coralie and Dash zooming around, both of them going too fast to search the area closely.

"Oh, this is *squid-iculous*. We're never going to find them!" they heard Coralie say. "I give up. Should we say we give up, Dash?"

The dolphin whistled in response.

Kai and the others looked at each other. He motioned upward with his eyes, and they all nodded. He mouthed, "One ... two ... THREE!"

On THREE, they burst out of the center of the sponges, sending seaweed flying everywhere, just as Coralie and Dash were racing past. Coralie squealed, and Dash turned a somersault in surprise. Seaweed landed on top of them.

Coralie dissolved into giggles and grabbed handfuls of it, throwing them at Marina and Kai. Soon, the whole group was caught up in a seaweed fight. They only stopped when they were all covered in it and laughing so much that they could barely stay upright in the water.

"Playing with seaweed!" said a snooty voice. "You're such babies."

Glenda came swimming past with a gray-and-white porpoise on a harness. Although very similar to dolphins, porpoises are smaller and slimmer with slightly more pointed noses.

"What do you think of my new pet?" said Glenda proudly. "His name is Silver."

Kai frowned. "Isn't he from the training school?" The guard porpoises wore harnesses just like the one Silver had on.

"Yep. Watch this!" Glenda had a whistle made from a seashell tied on a seaweed ribbon around her neck. She unclipped Silver's leash from his harness, lifted the whistle to her mouth, and blew. Instantly, Silver swam in front of her, eyes eager.

Glenda blew three more blasts on her whistle. Silver raced off through the water until another blast made him stop in his tracks. He looked around, grabbed a surprised crab in his mouth, and carried it back to Glenda. He put it into her outstretched hand. He'd carried it so gently that he hadn't made even the tiniest scratch on the crab's shell with his teeth.

Glenda took it smugly but didn't give Silver even the smallest pat. Silver looked confused and nudged her hand, seeking praise. "Isn't he clever—and so obedient?" Glenda said, ignoring him.

"Yes, he is, but that's because he's been trained by the guards!" Kai exclaimed. "He's a working animal, not a pet."

Glenda blew a long blast on the whistle and nodded to the right. Silver set off in that direction. He circled around the others, and with little nudges of his head, started to herd them toward Glenda.

"What's he doing?" gasped Coralie.

"Rounding you up!" Glenda giggled as Silver gave Kai a particularly hard push, sending him flying forward. "He'll easily win the most talented pet competition. You have no chance. No chance at all!"

"But that's not fair!" Coralie burst out. "You only got a guard porpoise because your dad is the Chief Guard."

Marina nodded. "You didn't train him, Glenda. That's basically cheating."

"And do I look like I care?" Glenda smirked. "There's nothing in the rules that says you have to have trained the pet yourself. My father checked. What's that?" She pointed over their heads. They looked around in confusion, and she laughed. "Oh, it's just your hope of winning any prizes disappearing into the distance. Not that your useless pets would have stood a chance anyway!" And with that she flounced off, Silver swimming obediently beside her.

"I can't believe her!" exploded Coralie.

Naya nodded. "It might not be against the rules, but I think it's really wrong to enter a pet into the competition that you haven't trained yourself."

"She's right, though," said Kai gloomily. "We're never going to beat her now."

"We might!" Marina exclaimed. "We can still come up with something *krill-iant*!" Her eyes narrowed and she looked thoughtful. "The question is—what?"

Chapter Four
A Daring Plan

For the next five mornings, as soon as Kai and Marina woke up, they swam to the whirlpool. Marina was relieved when every day they found a white stone with an "M" lying on the rocks beside the whirlpool. However, on the sixth day, they hunted everywhere but couldn't find a stone waiting for them.

"Maybe your dad hasn't had a chance to throw one into the whirlpool yet today," Kai suggested as he, Marina, Sammy, and Tommy scoured the rocks.

Marina looked anxious. "Maybe."

"You know what he's like when he's studying something exciting," said Kai, trying to make his friend feel better. "I bet he's been up all night working and just fell asleep."

Marina forced a smile. "You're probably right. I hope he's having a good time and getting a lot of research done. We can come back later."

Kai nodded. "I'm sure we'll find a stone then."

They headed back to the cave and had breakfast—seaweed toast and sweet sea plums, Kai's favorite—and then they met up with the others. They all decided to clean up litter in the reef. Although Mermaids Rock was a long way from land, plastic waste still washed up in the reef and caused a lot of problems for the sea creatures.

"Let's see who can pick up the most litter in 10 minutes," suggested Coralie.

"Okay." Kai nudged Marina. "That sounds

fun, doesn't it?"

"Mmm," she said, looking distracted. He was sure she was thinking about her dad.

"Bet Tommy and I can beat you and Sammy!" he said, hoping to get her attention.

His plan worked.

"Oh, no, you can't!" Marina said.

"Is everyone ready?" said Coralie. "When you pick up litter, bring it back here, and we'll see who has the most after 10 minutes. On your mark ... get set ... GO!"

They raced away across the reef. Kai and Tommy found three plastic bottles, two plastic bags, and some fishing net. "I bet we have enough to win," Kai said as he and Tommy whooshed up to their pile of litter at the end of 10 minutes.

But when they added up everyone's piles of litter, it was Naya and Octavia who had won. They had collected 20 pieces of plastic! Octavia waved her arms at everyone in delight.

"I guess it helps having eight arms!" said Naya.

"Hang on. I'm sure I collected that piece of plastic," said Marina, pointing to a red bottle. "Did you take it from my pile, Octavia?"

Octavia covered her head with her arms and shook as if she were laughing.

"You cheated!" exclaimed Marina.

"I'm really sorry," gasped Naya. "Octavia, that was very naughty!"

Octavia's dark eyes twinkled mischievously, and she shot away in a cloud of black ink.

"I'm sorry, everyone!" Naya apologized. "I thought we'd won fair and square."

"It's okay," said Marina. "The important thing is that we picked up the litter before any sea creatures tried to eat it or got tangled in it."

"I hate that creatures in the reef get injured by this stuff," said Luna. "I wish there was some magic we could use that would make it go away."

Kai started to put the garbage into the large seaweed sack they had brought with them. Luna swam over to help him.

"I wonder if there's any plastic in the Arctic," Luna said. Marina heaved a sigh, and he knew she was thinking about her dad again.

"Why don't we do some training with our pets?" said Kai quickly. "We need to figure out what they're doing for the talent show."

"We really do," agreed Coralie. "We can't let Glenda win."

"High five, Tommy!" said Kai, trying out a new trick he'd been teaching him. He held his hand up, but instead of slapping it, Tommy rolled over onto his back and waggled his flippers.

"Not a very high five!" Coralie grinned.

"I've been teaching Octavia to put my braids into a neat bun," said Naya. "Octavia, come back here and show everyone!" she called.

Octavia swam up behind her. Her arms moved fast in Naya's hair.

"Um, Naya, are you sure that's what you wanted her to do?" said Marina, frowning.

Naya felt her hair with her hands as Octavia swam back to admire her work. Her long hair was now tangled into one big clump.

"I don't think hairdressing is Octavia's talent," said Kai.

Naya groaned. "Maybe not!"

"What about Melly? Can she do anything?" Coralie asked Luna.

"Actually, I have been teaching her a trick," said Luna. She called her manatee over. "Melly! Play dead!"

Melly immediately rolled over onto her back and went very still.

"That's really good, Luna," said Kai, impressed.

"Thanks." Luna looked happy. "Good job, Melly! You can roll back now."

They all waited, but Melly didn't move.

"Melly?" said Luna uncertainly.

The manatee snored.

"She fell asleep!" Coralie giggled. "Oh, dear! She'd better not do that in the show, Luna!"

"This is useless!" said Kai. "None of us is going to be able to beat Glenda and Silver."

"We just need to keep practicing," said Naya.

"You can," said Marina, "but I'm going to the whirlpool again to see if there's a stone from Dad."

"Wait, we'll come with you," said Kai, not wanting her to go alone.

They swam to Mermaids Rock, but there was still no white pebble with an "M" on it.

Marina looked worried. "Do you think my dad is in trouble?"

"Not necessarily. After all, there isn't a red stone," Naya said, trying to comfort her.

"He could just be tracking walruses and has gone too far from the whirlpool to throw a stone into it," suggested Coralie.

"Or he could have been distracted by

something exciting and forgotten about the stones," Kai pointed out.

"I'm sure he's fine, Marina," said Luna, squeezing her hand.

Marina bit her lip. "I hope so."

Marina swam back to the whirlpool three more times that day, but still no stone appeared. When one didn't appear the following day either, she began to get seriously worried.

"Dad wouldn't have forgotten for two days," Marina said to Kai. "Something is definitely wrong."

The pets crowded around, trying to make Marina feel better—Melly, Tommy, and Dash rubbed their heads against her, Octavia smoothed her hair, and Sammy snuggled into her neck.

Marina looked at the whirlpool. "I think I should go to the Arctic and try to find him."

"We're not supposed to use the whirlpool without permission," Naya reminded her.

"We've done it before," said Marina. "And there are no guards here today. I bet we could get there and back without anyone knowing."

"But your dad said it could be dangerous," protested Luna.

"I know. But if he's in trouble, I need to help him!" said Marina. "I have to go. I'll see you later." She pushed the animals away gently and went to the edge of the whirlpool.

"Wait! You can't go alone!" said Kai quickly.

"We'll come with you!" said Coralie and Naya.

"You don't have to," Marina said.

"If you're going to be crushed by an iceberg, then we'll be crushed by one, too!" Coralie declared.

Luna looked alarmed at the thought, but she nodded hard. "Definitely."

"Don't even think about trying to stop us!" said Kai fiercely. "We're coming with you, and that's that!"

"Thanks," Marina said, her face breaking into a smile. "You're the best friends ever!"

"Before we go, we should get some supplies," said Naya, her eyes glinting with excitement. "Marina, why don't you go back to your cave and see if your dad left any Fire Potion bottles there—we'll each need to drink them so we don't freeze. I'll go and get some of my hand-warming clamshells and one of my emergency lanterns."

"I'll grab a first-aid kit in case we need it!" said Kai.

"And Luna and I can get some food," added Coralie.

Marina looked much happier now that they were actually going to do something. "Great! Let's meet back here as soon as we can."

Kai turned a somersault in the water. They were going on another adventure. Operation Arctic Rescue was about to begin!

Chapter Five
Arctic Adventure

A little while later, the group met back at the whirlpool. Naya had a seaweed bag across her body. It was stuffed with things she thought they might need. Kai passed her the first-aid kit, and Coralie added some seaweed cookies. Marina had five Fire Potion bottles that she'd found in a box in her dad's study. She handed them out.

Kai tilted the little bottle back and forth and watched the powder move. What was it going to taste like?

They opened the lids and let seawater in. Then they refastened them and shook the bottles until the powder dissolved and the bottles were filled with a fizzing bright red liquid.

"Is everyone ready to drink them?" said Marina. "Let's do it together."

"Wait! What about the pets? Won't they need some, too?" Luna asked anxiously. "Manatees like Melly can't survive in really cold water, and I'm sure it won't be much good for any of the animals—they're used to living in warm water. Can we share our potion with them?"

"Of course! I'm sure it'll be fine to share," said Marina. She took the lid off the bottle and gave Sammy a drop. He licked it up, and then jumped around and spun in a circle.

The other animals reacted in the same way when they had some.

"Okay, now it's our turn," said Marina, gulping down the rest of hers.

Kai copied her. The liquid fizzed and bubbled on his tongue. It was both sweet and salty. As he swallowed, he felt a fiery warmth spreading across his throat and down into his tummy. His tail fin twitched and began to tingle. He suddenly felt as if he were glowing all over. "Jumping jellyfish!" he said. "I feel very strange!"

"I'm really warm," said Luna, holding her long, dark-red hair up and fanning her face.

"I'm definitely ready to jump into some freezing water!" said Coralie.

"Then what are we waiting for? Let's go!" cried Marina. "Take us to the Arctic," she told the whirlpool. "To north of Baffin Bay!"

The whirlpool began to swirl faster, and they dove into the frothing foam. As the waters closed over Kai's head, he felt himself starting to spin. Bright stars exploded around him, and the water flashed through every shade of blue—turquoise to aquamarine to indigo to sky blue to lilac blue. Kai spun faster and faster until the whirlpool flung him out.

Opening his eyes, he saw that he was next to the others in a clear patch of dark blue and green water. He was very glad that he'd had the Fire Potion—the water looked freezing cold, but with the magic liquid inside him, he felt tingly and warm.

Tommy swam up and stuck his head uncertainly under Kai's arm. Octavia wrapped her arms around Naya, Melly pushed against Luna, and Sammy hid in Marina's hair. Even with the Fire Potion, it was clear that they felt uncomfortable being in an environment that was so different from the warm, tropical waters they usually lived in. Only Dash looked reasonably happy, but then dolphins were able to live in much colder waters than the other animals.

Glancing down, Kai noticed that the bottom of the ocean was rocky—the craggy boulders covered sparsely with lichen and brown seaweed. A couple of sea jellies bobbed past them, but otherwise, they were alone.

"It's weird here," said Kai, thinking of their coral reef that was so full of life, movement, and color. "There's hardly anything in the water."

"It's not as dark as I thought it would be," said Naya. "I thought the ice on the surface would block out more light than this." She glanced up. "Hang on. That's odd. There isn't any ice overhead! But the ocean should be frozen...."

"Let's go up to the surface and look around," Marina suggested.

As they burst out of the water, Kai blinked. They were swimming in the mouth of the bay, and the light above them was blinding. The Sun's rays bounced off the pieces of ice that were floating across the ocean. Nearby, there was an enormous, glistening iceberg made out of turquoise-and-white ice. It had a flat top and a large tunnel through its sides, almost big enough for a boat to sail through.

Looking behind him, Kai saw dark
mountains that sloped down to a rocky beach.
Where the beach met the ocean, there was
a strip of thick sea ice jutting out over the
water. It looked like it had once been thicker,
but now chunks of it had broken off and were
floating around in the bay. Another smaller
iceberg was still attached to the sea ice at one
end of the bay, but it looked as if it would soon
break away and float free, too, to drift along
on the ocean currents.

"Oh, bubbles!" breathed Luna, gazing around. "I've never been anywhere like this."

"It's awesome," said Kai, taking in the shining, icy landscape.

"*Clam-tastic!*" agreed Coralie.

Two large white seabirds with black patches on the top of their heads flew above them, calling to each other with eerie cries.

"Arctic terns," said Naya, pointing.

Dash whistled eagerly, and Coralie nodded. "All right, Dash, go and explore—see if you can find any clues as to where Marina's dad is." The dolphin raced off across the sea, leaping out of the water and arching over the surface before plunging back in as he headed for the larger iceberg.

"I wonder where Dad is," said Marina, looking around.

"Um ... everyone," said Naya. "I don't want to alarm you, but the ice really shouldn't be like this at this time of year. There should be a much larger platform of solid sea ice reaching out to here, not open water that we can swim in. The spring thaw must have started a lot earlier than your dad expected, Marina."

"Didn't he say that the waters would be dangerous once the ice started to melt?" said Luna.

Marina nodded uneasily. "He said there would be whales and boats and other things."

The sound of a horn blasting out across the water made them all jump. They swung around. There was a ship sailing slowly through the open waters some distance away. It was heading toward them.

"Quick! Hide!" gasped Naya. "We can't let them see us!"

They dove under the water, and Kai saw a sight that sent fear shooting down his spine. An enormous black whale with a white patch was swimming right at them!

"Orca!" he yelled as it loomed closer. Not so long ago, on a different adventure, they'd been chased by three vicious orcas, or killer whales. It had been really scary, and they had barely escaped! He turned to swim away.

"Wait, Kai! It's a bowhead whale, not an orca!" Marina shouted, grabbing his arm. "It won't harm us—at least not on purpose. It could squash us without meaning to, though. Let's get out of its way!"

They scattered as the enormous whale swam through the water where they had just been swimming. It barely even registered that they were there and headed silently upward, blowing a fountain of water out through its blowhole as it reached the surface. Watching it more closely, Kai could see that it did look different from an orca—there was less white on its body, and it didn't have a dorsal fin on its back. It was also bigger. He was very glad that bowheads were friendly.

Coralie nudged him. "Hey, Kai, what did the whale say to his friend when he asked him over for dinner?" she whispered as they watched the whale continue its journey to the open sea beyond the bay.

"What?" said Kai.

"Whale-come to my house!"

Kai chuckled, the panic he'd been feeling earlier fading. "That's definitely not one of your best, Coralie! Come on. Let's go and see if the boat is still there."

They risked poking their heads out again. The whale had come to the surface, and they could see the people on the boat taking photographs of it as it swam past them toward the open ocean. The boat turned and followed it.

"The people have gone after the whale!" Kai said in relief.

"Phew!" said Marina. "Now we can look for my dad. He wanted to come to this bay because it has the largest walrus population in this part of the Arctic, so keep an eye out for walruses. Dad will probably be somewhere close to them!"

Dash came swimming back through the ocean, as fast as a silver arrow. He reared up in the water, whistling and clapping his flippers. He glanced back the way he'd come and motioned toward the enormous, flat-topped iceberg with his snout.

"What is it?" Coralie said. He whistled again. "He's telling us to go with him. I think there's something by the iceberg he wants us to see."

"Maybe it's Dad!" gasped Marina, setting off through the water toward it. The others raced after her. Coralie and Dash overtook her and reached the iceberg first.

It was immediately clear that the piece of the iceberg they could see above the surface of the water was only a very small part of it. They swam down, exploring its jagged, icy sides.

It was like an enormous underwater building made of ice. There were cracks and crevices and holes big enough to swim through.

Dash led the way to a cave opening and whistled eagerly.

Coralie looked inside. "Marina! Your dad's things are here. This must be the place he's been using as his base!"

They went into the cave. It was larger than they'd imagined. Inside, they could see Marina's dad's backpack, a pot of flickering mermaid fire, his pouch of white pebbles, a bag of Fire Potion bottles, and his research notes.

"But where's Dad?" said Marina.

Tommy tugged at Kai's arm and swam to a smaller opening in the cave wall. It seemed to be an icy tunnel. Tommy sniffed, and before Kai could stop him, he zoomed off down the tunnel headfirst. Kai heard his shell banging against the tunnel walls a few times and then, to his relief, the turtle came shooting out into the water underneath the cave entrance.

"It's an ice slide!" said Kai in surprise.

"Maybe Dad left something in there," said Marina.

"I'll check!" said Kai.

He dove into the tunnel headfirst like Tommy had and whooshed down, slipping from side to side on the watery surface and catapulting out beside Tommy. There were no clues as to where Marina's dad was, but it was fun!

Kai swam back to the cave entrance. Sammy had been bobbing around the walls of the cave, and now he wrapped his tail around a thick lock of Marina's hair and tugged her toward one wall, his horns waggling.

"What is it?" Marina asked, reaching out to touch the walls. "Look! Marks in the ice! I think Dad has been keeping track of the days. He's carved a line into the ice each day." She counted. "He's made five lines."

"But your dad's been here seven days," Naya pointed out, picking up the research notes.

Marina frowned. "So why are there only five marks?"

Kai had a worrying thought. "He sent you five pebbles and then stopped, didn't he? Maybe he hasn't been here in this cave for the last two days. Maybe something happened to him when he was out doing research."

"Don't worry—we'll find him," Coralie said quickly as Marina looked alarmed.

"The notes he made are about a large herd of female walruses and their calves," said Naya, looking up from the research papers she was leafing through. "The herd is bound to be close to land if there are babies."

"Let's try to find them!" said Coralie.

As they left the cave, Kai glanced back. His eyes fell on the Fire Potion bottles in the bag. "Marina, your dad said he needed to have a bottle of Fire Potion every day, didn't he?"

She nodded, and he saw her eyes widen as she realized what he was thinking. "If he's in trouble, he might not have had any for two days. We need to find him—and fast!"

Chapter Six
Stampede!

The friends swam across the surface of the icy water toward the rocky beach. The closer they got to the land, the harder it was to swim because the ice floes were packed more tightly together. They had to swim around them, searching the stretches of clear water.

"Walruses!" said Luna, pointing to a nearby ice floe. "But that's not a very big herd, is it?"

Eight very large, round, brown adult walruses with long yellow tusks were crammed together on the floating platform of ice. There wasn't a spare inch of space—the walruses were resting their heads on each other's backs and honking loudly as the floe drifted slowly on the current.

"That's a group of males," said Naya. "They're huge, and if they were female, they would have babies with them. They probably don't live in the bay but are just traveling north to where the ice is thicker. I don't think they are the ones that Marina's dad was studying. His notes were all about a large herd of mothers and calves."

"Like that herd over there?" said Luna, pointing to the land.

Kai squinted and then realized that what he had thought was a rocky beach was in fact a huge herd of mother and baby walruses, tightly squashed together.

"Look at them!" Coralie said in astonishment.

"What do they eat?" Kai asked rather

nervously. Some of the walruses were seriously big—three times as large as him—and those long yellow tusks looked very scary. There were so many of them that he hoped they didn't like eating merpeople!

"Their favorite food is clams," said Naya. "They like to feed off shellfish beds in the shallow water."

"They're so cute," breathed Luna.

Kai wasn't sure that cute was the right word. As they swam closer, he could see that the walruses were very round and blubbery, with almost no hair. Their bodies were a mottled pink-brown color, their dark eyes were hidden by wrinkles of skin, and they had long, bristly whiskers on their muzzles. The babies were pretty cute, though. They were about three feet long, with scrunched-up faces. They were crawling all over their moms, snuggling under their flippers and rubbing their heads against their mothers' sides. Some of them were on the beach, while others were on the remaining strip of solid sea ice that extended out from the beach and hadn't yet broken up. A cacophony of noisy honks and bellows echoed across the water.

Coralie giggled. "Hey, I thought of a joke."

"Spare us!" begged Kai.

Coralie ignored them. "What do mommy

walruses say when their babies cry?"

They all looked at her.

"Don't blubber!" She swam away with a grin before they could flick water at her.

"Look at that huge walrus," Kai said, pointing to a giant mother walrus. She was easily the biggest and was nursing a small baby on the ice.

"Her baby looks like one of the youngest," said Naya. "Only about—" She was interrupted by the sound of a ship's horn blowing across the bay.

Turning, Kai saw that the ship from earlier had given up chasing the whale and was now heading toward the beach so that the passengers could get some photographs of the walruses. It couldn't get very close because of the thick ice, but it was still close enough to startle the mothers. They started to trumpet in alarm.

The horn honked again, and the walruses began to drag themselves across the rocks and ice toward the water, their bellies bumping on the ground and their flippers flapping.

"It's a walrus stampede!" gasped Naya as the panicking walruses slid and dove into the water.

Some of the mothers grabbed their babies, disappearing down to the bottom and swimming under the thick layer of ice. But other calves weren't so lucky. As the larger walruses at the back bulldozed their way through, some of the little ones were sent flying. They went rolling across the ice and splashed into the water.

"Oh, the poor babies!" cried Luna.

"Let's help them!" said Coralie, diving forward.

"No!" Naya grabbed her. "We'll get hurt if we try to go over there now. We have to wait until they calm down."

"I hope my dad didn't get caught in a stampede," said Marina anxiously.

With the walruses now in the ocean, the people on the boat got bored, and it sailed back to the open water. The walruses started to haul themselves out of the water and flap their way back across the ice, the mothers calling loudly as they tried to find their babies. Luckily, none of the herd seemed badly hurt, although a few had scrapes and cuts. One by one, each mother and baby pair was reunited until only the giant walrus was left. She heaved herself around on the ice, honking anxiously.

"Oh, no! That big one has lost her baby!" said Luna.

"Maybe it's still in the water," said Kai. "Let's see if we can find it!"

They dove down and swam under the ice. The water was shallower here but darker because of the thick ice overhead. "Did you bring your emergency lantern?" Kai said to Naya.

"Yes. Here you go," she said, fishing a glass jar out of her bag. It had mermaid powder in the bottom with a tiny bag of liquid on top. She shook it hard so that the bag burst open onto the powder, and as the two elements mixed together, the jar flared with light. Naya held it up in front of her. Light shone out of it, but it was still difficult to see much in the gloom.

Dash turned around in front of them and waved his flippers as if telling them to stay back. "What is it?" Coralie frowned.

Dash swam on a few strokes and then looked back. He shook his head at them as they followed him. "He seems to want to go on alone," said Coralie, puzzled.

"Maybe he's going to use his echolocation to try to find the baby!" said Naya.

Dolphins like Dash could send out sound waves by making clicks with their tongues. As the sound waves traveled through the water, they hit objects and bounced back, and a part of Dash's brain could figure out where those objects were.

"Go on, Dash!" urged Coralie. "See if you can find the baby."

Dash nudged Tommy. "He wants Tommy to go with him," said Coralie.

"I bet it's because Tommy is really good at smelling things," said Kai. "Tommy might be able to find the baby by its scent." He patted Tommy encouragingly. "Go, Tommy!"

Dash and Tommy disappeared into the gloom, and the others waited anxiously. Each minute seemed to drag by, but at last Dash and Tommy came racing back. Tommy waved his flippers, and Dash whistled urgently.

"They found something!" cried Coralie.

"Is it the walrus baby?" Kai asked.

Tommy and Dash nodded and shot away.

Chapter Seven
Operation Rescue

Dash led the way under the ice, down to the rocky ocean floor. There were cracks between the rocks and boulders—some wide enough for a mermaid to wriggle through, others so narrow that only a flipper would fit. Naya held up her emergency lantern, and its glow illuminated the dark.

Dash and Tommy swam over to two large boulders.

"Look!" gasped Coralie, pointing. "The baby! It's stuck between those rocks!"

The baby walrus was trapped on its back, its little round body tightly wedged in the crack. It was making bleating sounds, and its short whiskers quivered. It looked terrified.

"Luna," said Marina quickly. "Can you calm it down?"

Luna started to hum softly. As the baby listened to her humming, it stopped struggling, and the panic left its eyes. She rubbed its chest, and it visibly relaxed, its bleating turning to a quiet whimper. "Don't worry," she said gently. "We'll get you out and take you back to your mother."

The baby looked at her with complete trust. She wriggled her fingers under its head. "Can you come and help me get it out?" she called to the others. She started to hum again to keep the baby calm as they came over.

"It's wedged in so tightly," said Marina as she squeezed her fingers underneath it. They pulled, but the baby didn't move.

Octavia shot over, leaving a trail of bubbles behind her. She slid her eight slim, strong arms between the rock and the baby, and then she gave a sharp tug backward. The baby emerged from the crack like a cork popping out of a bottle.

It turned a
somersault and started
waggling its plump
little body. It swam up
to Luna and rubbed
its bristly nose
against her cheek,
then put its front
flippers around
her neck and
smiled at the others.
It didn't look injured.

"You're adorable," Luna said, hugging
it. "Now, let's get you back to your poor mom.
She's really worried about you."

When they swam out from under the ice
sheet, they could still see the huge mother
walrus flapping frantically around the ice,
calling for her baby. A couple of other walruses
who were lying near the edge of the ice sheet
saw them and started to trumpet in alarm.

Luna began to hum. The last thing they wanted was for the walruses to stampede again.

As her humming reached the animals, their eyes relaxed, and they stopped giving loud cries of alarm. Luna and the others helped the baby wriggle out of the water and onto the ice before pulling themselves out. They sat on the ice and dangled their tails in the water while the baby lifted its head and bleated loudly.

Somehow, despite the general noise, its mother heard it. She swung around and came galloping across the ice, bellowing and shoving the other walruses out of the way in her rush to get to her baby.

For a horrible moment, Kai thought she was going to crash right into them. "Watch out!" he shouted, slipping into the water and pulling Coralie and Luna with him as the enormous, solid mother bore down on them. Marina and Naya jumped in, too, but just in time, the mother slid to a halt.

The baby wriggled over to her, and she grabbed it in her flippers, flopped onto her back, and hugged it tightly to her chest. It wriggled in delight and covered her face with whiskery kisses. Then it pointed with a flipper to Kai and the others watching from the edge of the sea ice. The mother walrus carefully put her baby down and approached them. She peered down at them, her small eyes blinking in her wrinkled face.

"Hello," said Luna softly, reaching up. Tilting her head so that her tusks were safely out of the way, the mother walrus rubbed her forehead against Luna's hand. Then she dove into the water with a splash.

"What's she doing?" exclaimed Coralie as the mother swam around them, touching their tails with her whiskers.

"I have no idea," said Marina.

The mother poked her head out of the water and made a questioning noise. "Crrk?"

"I'm sorry. We don't understand walrus," Luna said helplessly.

"Crrk? Crrk?" The mother walrus nudged their tails, and then jerked her head toward the flat-topped iceberg that was floating out in the bay. Then she nodded at the nearby smaller iceberg that was still attached to the sea ice.

"She's trying to tell us something," said Kai.

"I think she's telling us that she's seen another merperson," said Luna suddenly. "That's why she keeps nudging our tails!"

"Maybe she's seen Dad!" gasped Marina.

Kai watched as the walrus motioned toward the smaller iceberg again with her head. "She could be trying to say that she's seen another merperson over there!"

"Crrk!" said the walrus.

"Oh, thank you!" Marina cried.

She set off toward the iceberg, swimming as fast as she could. This one had a pointy top and was made from blue-and-green ice. It was smaller than the other iceberg, but even so, it still looked like a mini mountain, its jagged sides reaching deep into the water. Marina started swimming around it. "Dad? Dad?" she called desperately.

The others joined in. "Mr. Silverfin! Are you here?"

Kai thought hard. Where could Marina's dad be? Why wasn't he answering? As his eyes fell on Tommy swimming beside him, he had an idea. "Tommy, can you find Marina's dad? Find Marina's dad!"

Tommy understood "Find." He dove down into the water and began to glide around the uneven sides of the iceberg, investigating the holes and crevices. He swam farther and farther down, and after a few minutes came shooting back to Kai. His eyes were worried. He grabbed Kai's arm gently in his mouth and started to tug him along.

"I think Tommy may have found

something!" Kai called. Everyone raced over and followed Tommy through the water. Suddenly, the turtle lowered his head and charged at a thin crack in the side of the iceberg. He thumped into the ice with his hard head.

"What are you doing, Tommy?" Kai exclaimed. "You're going to hurt yourself!"

Tommy ignored him and charged again until a chunk of ice broke away from the crack.

Marina swam over and peered through the hole. "It's Dad! He's inside the iceberg!" She swung around, an alarmed look in her eyes. "I don't know how he got in there, but I can see a hole behind the ice, and he's in there, lying down. Dad! Dad!" She began to bang on the iceberg. "Can you hear me?"

The others joined her. Through the hole, Kai could see Marina's dad lying motionless on the cave floor. Everyone thumped on the icy sides, and Tommy thwacked the ice again with his head, but Marina's dad didn't move, and the ice wouldn't break.

"What are we going to do?" Marina cried desperately. "We have to get my dad out of there right away!"

Chapter Eight
One Good Turn

"There must be a way to get inside!" Marina cried desperately.

"I could go back to the reef through the whirlpool and try to make something to melt the ice," Naya suggested.

"Or we go back and get the guards to come and break through the ice with their tridents," suggested Kai.

"There isn't time!" Marina burst out. Kai had never seen Marina cry before, but now her eyes filled with tears. "Dad looks really sick and cold."

A trumpeting noise made them look around. The gigantic mother walrus appeared in the water behind them, her baby swimming beside her.

Luna swam over. "Thank you for helping us find Marina's dad," she said, petting them.

The two walruses watched as Tommy charged at the ice and bounced off, and the friends tried to pull chunks of ice away. The mother walrus pushed her baby into Luna's arms and then swam forward, softly nudging the others out of the way.

"What are you doing?" Marina asked her.

In reply, the mother plunged her sharp tusks into the ice where the crack was. The ice splintered with a loud *CRACK!* as her tusks sheared through it.

Naya gasped. "She's helping us!"

They were all focused on watching the walrus when Luna cried, "Wait! Where's Melly going?" The manatee had suddenly swum off and didn't stop as Luna called after her. Melly usually swam slowly, but now she put on a burst of speed and sped away from them, her round body waggling through the water. Luna looked anxious. "Where did she go?"

"I don't know, but I'm sure she'll be back soon," said Kai. He turned to the iceberg. They could go and look for Melly later if she didn't return. Right now, they had to concentrate on Marina's dad.

"Do that again—please!" Marina begged the mother.

CRACK!

This time, huge chunks of ice fell away, making a bigger hole. One final blow from her enormous, sharp tusks, and the hole was big enough for them to get inside the iceberg. The walrus moved back as Marina dove into the ice cave. She touched her father's forehead. "He's freezing, but he's still alive!" she cried in relief.

Kai, Naya, and Coralie plunged into the cave and helped her carry her dad. As they got him out of the ice, the mother walrus swam underneath him and gently pushed him upward. Reaching the surface, she used her head to lift him onto the sea ice. Marina and the others pulled themselves out beside him.

"Dad! Dad!" cried Marina, shaking his shoulders. Her dad's face was pale, and his silver tail had turned gray. "He's so cold!"

"He needs some Fire Potion," said Naya. "We should have brought some with us from the other cave."

"Dash and I could go back and get some—" Coralie started to say, but she was interrupted by a splash and Melly suddenly appearing. Opening her mouth, the manatee spat a small bottle half filled with red powder onto the ice.

"Melly! You're so clever!" gasped Luna. She hugged the manatee. "She must have remembered seeing the Fire Potion with your dad's things and realized we were going to need it."

"Oh, thank you, Melly!" gasped Marina, quickly unscrewing the top. "It's exactly what we need." She added some seawater and shook it. The red liquid fizzed and bubbled. Lifting her dad's head, Marina poured it little by little into his mouth. "Come on, Dad," she begged. "Drink this and wake up. Please!"

Nothing happened. Each second stretched into what felt like a minute, and Marina grew more and more worried. But suddenly, her dad coughed and spluttered and blinked his eyes open. "Marina?" he croaked in surprise.

"Yes, I'm here!" she said, grabbing his hand.

Her dad started to shiver. "I'm s-so cold!" His teeth chattered. "I feel warm inside now, but s-still so c-cold on the outside."

Marina rubbed his bare arms. "If only we had a blanket," she said to the others.

The baby walrus wriggled onto the ice. It lay down next to Marina's dad, cuddling in as close as it could. With a grunt, the mother heaved herself out of the water and hauled herself over to Marina's dad, too. She flopped down on the other side of him, her enormous body dwarfing him. She pushed herself as close as she could to him and laid her head gently on his chest. He looked surprised but was too weak and cold to do anything other than lie still.

"What are they doing?" Coralie said in astonishment.

"They're snuggling up to him to warm him up!" Naya said. "Like they do with each other."

"And it's working!" said Kai, seeing color coming back into Marina's dad's face. "He's looking better already."

Naya opened her bag and pulled out the shell hand warmers. "Here, everyone. Activate these. They'll help, too!"

They added seawater to the bags in the shells and then shut them. The shells started to heat up. Marina placed them in her dad's hands and around his head.

Soon, he stopped shivering, and his tail turned from gray to silver. He coughed and started to sit up. The mother walrus moved her head off his chest, but she kept her warm body close to his.

"I feel better," he said, sounding relieved. "So much warmer. Thank you—all of you." He rubbed the walrus and her baby.

"What happened?" asked Marina. "How did you end up inside the iceberg, Dad?"

"I was studying the mother and baby walruses when a ship disturbed them and they stampeded," he said.

"That happened when we were watching them, too," said Coralie.

"Unfortunately, I was on the sea ice at the time," said Marina's dad. "As they rushed into the water, they knocked me into the ocean, and I hit my head on the iceberg. I can't remember much after that. I just remember being in the water and seeing a wide crack and a hollowed-out space inside the iceberg. I pulled myself through the crack so I was out of the way of the walruses and then I must have passed out. I don't remember anything else. I imagine the iceberg must have shifted and the crack closed up, leaving me trapped inside."

Marina hugged him. "I'm so glad you're okay. I was really worried."

"I don't understand why you're here, though, or how you found me," said Marina's dad.

They quickly explained.

He smiled. "Well, I guess I shouldn't be encouraging you to use the whirlpool without permission, but I'm very glad you did."

"Will you come home with us now?" said Marina.

"Yes. It's too dangerous to do any more research here while the ice is breaking up," he said, petting the walruses. "It shouldn't be thawing so soon, but unfortunately, the world's climate is changing, meaning the ice melts earlier and earlier each year. That's bad news for creatures like these walruses, who depend on the ice."

Naya nodded. "I guess they have two choices. They can either travel north where there's always ice even in summer—but it's a very dangerous journey when their calves are so young—or they can stay here."

Marina's dad sighed. "The trouble is that the ice breaking up means more boatloads of humans fishing and visiting. If the human tourists see the walruses, they'll want to sail into the bay and take photographs, and that will cause stampedes and more injuries. I think it's one of the reasons why the walrus numbers are declining."

"Isn't there anything we can do to help them?" Marina asked.

Her dad shook his head. "Sadly, global warming is out of our control—it's a human problem, not a merperson one. If we could stop the boats from coming here and disturbing the walruses, that would help, but I can't see how we can do that."

Luna hugged the mother walrus. "I'm so sorry. I wish we could do something more," she said. "You've been so kind to us."

Something Marina's dad had said tugged at Kai's mind. He felt like there was something they could do, but he couldn't quite put his finger on it. *If the human tourists see the walruses, they'll want to sail into the bay and take photographs, and that will cause stampedes....*

"Let's get your things, Dad," said Marina, "and go back to the reef."

Her dad nodded and gave the walruses one last pet. "Thank you, my friends," he said softly. "I don't know why you helped me, but I'm very grateful."

"Crrk!" said the mother walrus, looking at Kai and the others.

"I think she's saying one good tern deserves

another!" said Coralie. "Get it? Tern—Arctic tern—like the seabird we saw?"

Marina's dad's lips twitched. "Glad to see your jokes haven't gotten any better, Coralie!"

Coralie grinned. "Really? Are you *shore* about that?"

Laughing, they slid off the ice and into the water. They grabbed Marina's dad's equipment from the large cave and then headed to the mini whirlpool that would return them to the reef. But as they reached it, they saw that it was spinning fast—just like it did when someone was traveling through it.

"Who's using it?" said Kai in astonishment. "Who's coming through from the reef?"

Chapter Nine
Mermaid Magic

Kai's mom, Indra, came shooting out of the swirling waters of the whirlpool, trident in her hand.

"Kai!" she exclaimed, looking very relieved when she saw him and the others. "All of you! What are you doing here? You know you're not allowed to use the whirlpool without permission. You're going to be in serious trouble if Chief Razeem finds out!"

"How did you know we were here, Mom?" Kai asked, giving her a hug. He felt bad for worrying her.

"When I couldn't find you and I realized the first-aid kit was gone, I had a feeling you might have come here to look for Marina's dad."

"We had to," said Marina. "I was sure Dad was in trouble."

"And she was right," said her dad, squeezing Marina's shoulder. "I was badly injured— unconscious, and trapped in an ice cave. If they hadn't come, I would have frozen to death, Indra."

"Are you all right now?" she asked anxiously.

"Yes, thanks to this brave bunch," said Marina's dad.

"And the walruses," added Luna.

"Mom!" Kai exclaimed as he looked at her trident. The vague feeling that there was something they could do to help the walruses suddenly exploded into a full-blown idea. "The guards use their tridents to cast cloaking spells on our piece of ocean so that people sailing

close to our reef don't notice us and also feel
the urge to sail away, don't they? Can you cast
cloaking spells in other places, too?"

Marina gasped, and he knew she'd realized
what his idea was.

His mom nodded. "Yes—why?"

"Well, could you cast a spell on this bay
so that any humans sailing by don't see the
walruses who live here, and then they'll just
keeping sailing on? If they don't come into
the bay in their boats, then the walruses won't
stampede and injure their babies," said Kai.

"That could actually work!" said Marina's dad,
looking excited. "What a great idea, Kai! This
is the largest group of Atlantic walruses in the
Arctic. If they can live peacefully here without
disturbance, then their numbers might increase."

"We may not be able to stop global warming,
but we can help the walruses in the bay by doing
this!" said Naya, her eyes shining.

"Will you do it, Mom?" Kai asked.

She smiled. "Of course!"

They all swam to the mouth of the bay.
When they got there, they rose to the surface,
and Kai's mom moved her trident in a
complicated pattern, whispering the cloaking
spell as she did so. For a moment, the air in
the bay seemed to shiver. Then it settled, and
the bay looked normal—the floating ice; the
jagged, snow-topped mountains; the glittering
icebergs; and the walruses piled in mounds on
the ice and rocks.

"Now the walruses will be safe,"
said Kai's mom with a smile. "If any
ships come to the mouth of the bay, the
humans will see the walruses but will think
they're just rocks. They will also feel that there's
something strange about the bay, so they will
quickly sail on."

"And the walruses will be able to eat and sleep
and cuddle in peace!" said Coralie happily.

"Let's take one last look at them," said
Marina's dad.

They flicked their tails and swam toward the
herd. Some of the mothers were nursing their

babies or cuddling them. Others were diving into the water to find clams to eat, sometimes taking their babies with them on their backs. The air was full of the sounds of contented honks and bleats.

"They seem really happy," said Luna.

"I love the Arctic," said Kai, looking around at the shining water. The white of the icebergs stood out against the blue of the ocean, and the Arctic terns circled in the sky above them. At the mouth of the bay, he could see a pod of bowhead whales swimming north, their dark tail flukes breaking through the waves.

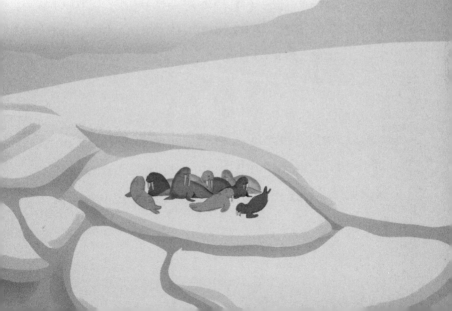

There would be narwhals traveling soon, too, and pure white beluga whales heading for the colder water. When autumn came and the ice formed again, the polar bears would return. Like the walruses, they would also benefit from the bay being undisturbed by curious humans. They would be able to hunt in peace and feed so that they could hibernate through the bitter winter.

"I hope it always stays like this," Kai went on. "I hope that the world doesn't heat up anymore."

"We all do," said his mom, squeezing his shoulder.

They took one last look at the happy herd of walruses before diving beneath the surface and swimming back to the whirlpool.

Kai, Luna, Marina, Coralie, and Naya shot out of the whirlpool with their pets by Mermaids Rock. As Kai turned himself the right way up, his heart sank. Chief Razeem was swimming nearby—his pointed black beard quivering, his eyes sharp. Glenda was beside him.

"I told you I saw them going through the whirlpool, Daddy!" she said triumphantly. "And that they were doing it without permission." She blinked her eyelashes and looked innocent. "I only told you because I was really worried about them."

"You five merchildren are in serious trouble!" snapped Chief Razeem, pointing at them. "What in Neptune's name do you think you're doing using the whirlpool without permission?"

Luckily, at that moment, Kai's mom and Marina's dad came through the whirlpool, too.

"It's okay, Chief

Razeem," Kai's mom said quickly. "The children were with me, and they had my permission to use the whirlpool."

"Why?" demanded Chief Razeem.

"I was in trouble in the Arctic," said Marina's dad. "They came to rescue me."

"We're all back safe and sound now, though," said Kai's mom briskly. "And the children have helped to protect a herd of walruses!"

Chief Razeem's anger faded. "Oh. Okay. Well … good job," he said gruffly.

Glenda's face fell. It was clear that she had been hoping they would be scolded and punished.

Kai's mom shepherded Kai and the others away. "Time to get some food. You must be starving."

"I really am!" said Coralie. "In fact, I'm so hungry, I could eat as much as a giant walrus!"

Kai grinned. "'Bye, Glenda," he called sweetly. "Thank you for being so concerned about us. We'll see you at the Spring Fair tomorrow."

Glenda glared at him and flounced away.

Chapter Ten
Show-stopping Pets

Although Kai had loved the glittering Arctic world, it felt really good to be back in the familiar, busy, warm waters of the coral reef. On his way to the Spring Fair, he swooped along with the shoals of tiny fish and hung on to Tommy's shell, letting the turtle tug him through the turquoise water, swerving around sea sponges and over beds of feathery anemones and sea star-covered rocks. Everywhere seemed so bright and colorful!

The fair was taking place near the school

and the Marine Sanctuary. There was a high slide made from coral, with a thick pile of bouncy purple-and-blue sea sponges at the bottom, and the area outside the school gates was packed with booths. There was one selling cupcakes filled with cream, one offering mermaid ice-cream sundaes, and others selling jewelry, hair clips, and ornaments made from shells and sea glass. There were also

competitions to enter—Kai guessed the weight of the triggerfish and how many shells there were in the jar, but the thing he was really looking forward to was the pet show!

Kai and Tommy met the others by the school gates. The five friends and their pets looked very excited. While they'd been eating a huge dinner at Kai's the night before, Marina had had a terrific idea for the contest.

"I can't wait for it to start!" she said now. "I hope my idea works and that we win!"

"Even if we don't, we'll have fun," said Kai.

They headed for the ring where the competition was taking place. Some of Kai's friends from school were already there with their pets.

"Hi, Rafi!" called Kai, waving at a boy who had a striped zebra moray eel around his shoulders.

"Hey, Pablo!" Pablo had a large leatherback turtle beside him.

His friends waved back.

"Look, there's Jazeela," said Naya, spotting Glenda's friend, who was holding a small pink sea star and looking bored.

"Out of my way! Move!" ordered a sharp voice. "My pet is very precious and expensive. Let me through!"

Marina rolled her eyes. "And here's Glenda."

Glenda swam into the ring. She had Silver,

her porpoise, with her, but he no longer had his harness on. She had swapped it for a collar and leash made of pink ribbon seaweed. Silver was pulling excitedly from side to side. "Stop that, Silver!" Glenda snapped as the porpoise darted toward Pablo's turtle. "Stop pulling me!"

"I thought Silver was really well trained," said Coralie in surprise as the porpoise towed Glenda around the ring.

Kai frowned. "Guard porpoises wear special harnesses when they're working. Mom told me that's because when they have their harness on, they know they have to behave. They're very clever and have a lot of energy. When they don't have their harness on, they think it's playtime and can be very naughty."

"I wonder if Glenda knows that...," said Luna slowly.

"Silver! Stop!" cried Glenda angrily as the porpoise pulled her over to say hello to the judge—an older, slightly severe-looking mermaid named Ms. Talia who worked with Luna's mom at the Marine Sanctuary. Glenda tried to pull him back, but he was too strong. He swam up enthusiastically, butting Ms. Talia on the nose.

"Ow!" gasped Ms. Talia. She rubbed her nose. "Glenda, please get your pet under control."

"I'm trying!" wailed Glenda as Silver shot off again, dragging her around the ring. "Stop it, you silly animal! Stop!"

But Silver was enjoying himself. He swam faster and faster and then charged out of the ring with Glenda clinging on to his leash. The nearby merpeople scattered as he tried to leap over the cupcake booth. Glenda let go of the leash at just the wrong moment and landed SPLAT on top of the cupcakes!

She sat up with cream all over her and screamed with fury as everyone burst out laughing. "I hate my pet!" she cried. "He can go back to the training school. I don't want him anymore!" Kai was sure he saw Silver give a wink before he turned a somersault and then set off as fast as he could back to the guards' training school.

Coralie's eyes sparkled mischievously. "Oh, Glenda! Don't say that. I'm sure he didn't embarrass you on *porpoise*!"

Glenda screamed at her, and Kai and Marina laughed so hard they had to clutch each other.

Ms. Talia clapped her hands for silence. "Well, that was an exciting if unexpected start to the competition," she said as Glenda's mother hurried a wailing Glenda away. "Now, let's see what talents these other pets have!"

Kai and the others watched and clapped as their friends from school showed off their pets. Rafi's zebra moray eel weaved around his tail and his arms and then tied itself into different types of knots. Pablo showed how his turtle

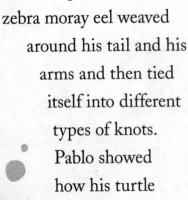

would let him ride balanced on its back. There were dolphins who turned acrobatic twists and somersaults, an octopus who could knit, and a lobster who danced solemnly in a circle!

The Save the Sea Creatures Club was the last act to perform. The friends swam out together. "We know this is supposed to be a talent contest for one pet, but we think our pets' main talent is working as a team," Marina announced, just as they had planned. "They're really clever and help us whenever we need them to. We put together a little play to show you what we mean."

Kai took over. He loved being in front of an audience. "Behold!" he said, sweeping his arm around the ring. "Before you, you see a young seahorse out for a swim in the coral reef, gathering important stones and shells for his young mermaid owner!"

Sammy bobbed into the center of the ring and picked up a stone with his tail. "One

day, he swims too far from his home and—
oh, no!—he finds himself in a dark cave...."
Octavia zoomed over and squirted out a sheet
of black ink, covering Sammy and hiding him
from sight, and then she shot back to the side.

"The poor little seahorse is lost and scared!"
cried Kai dramatically. "He doesn't know what
to do, but luckily, along come Tommy the
turtle and Dash the dolphin, the best search-
and-rescue team in the reef! With Dash's
echolocation and Tommy's sense of smell, they
find the little seahorse and bring him safely out
of the dark cave." Dash and Tommy slapped
flippers and swam into the cloud of ink.

A few moments later, they appeared
with Sammy between them. Then Octavia
polished him clean with her arms and hugged
him. "Cleaned and comforted by kind
Octavia, Sammy is ready to go home," said
Kai. "Luckily, Melly the manatee, with her
excellent memory, remembers where he lives

and returns him to his family, using her body to shelter him on the way."

Melly and Sammy swam out of the ring together, the little seahorse staying close to the large manatee's side.

"The end!" Kai announced, bowing as the audience clapped loudly.

Marina swam up beside Kai. "That's our made-up story," she told the audience. "But yesterday, our pets really did help us when we had to rescue a baby walrus and my dad."

"Dash used his echolocation to lead us to where the baby walrus was trapped," said Coralie.

"Octavia used her arms to free it," said Naya.

"Then Tommy used his amazing sense of smell to find Marina's dad when he was trapped inside an iceberg," put in Kai.

"And Melly remembered the bottles of Fire Potion she'd seen at his base and went to get one to help warm him up," said Luna.

"Sammy was clever enough to see the lines that Dad had made on the wall, which made us realize that he was in trouble. They worked together," said Marina.

"Just like us!" finished Kai with a grin. "Because that's when merpeople are at their strongest!" They high-fived, and the audience cheered and applauded loudly.

"Well," said Ms. Talia, swimming over to them, "that wasn't quite what I was expecting, but it was extremely good. Your message was excellent, and your pets are very talented indeed. Excellent job. I really would love to make you the winners, but sadly, as Marina said, this is a competition for one pet and his or her special talent."

"We don't mind," said Kai. "We just wanted everyone to know how clever our pets are."

"And how much we love them," added Marina as Sammy cuddled into her neck.

Everyone cheered again, and beaming

happily, they left the ring as Rafi's zebra moray eel was announced the winner.

"Even though you didn't win the prize, you're winners to me," said Kai's mom, who had been watching at the ring entrance with Marina's dad. She hugged Kai. "I'm so proud of all of you. You really do have a habit of saving the day!" Tommy nudged her hand with his head, and she chuckled. "Yes, you pets, too!" she said.

"I agree, and as a thank you for yesterday, I'd like to get you a special treat," said Marina's dad.

"I'm guessing it's not going to be cupcakes," said Kai with a grin, looking at the ruined cupcake booth.

Marina's dad smiled. "No, I'm afraid not. How about an ice-cream sundae instead?"

"Perfect! And while we eat them, we can start planning our next adventure!" said Marina in delight.

"What do you think we'll do next?" said Coralie.

"We've been to the deep reef, a kelp forest, the Arctic...," said Naya, checking the places off on her fingers.

Kai grabbed Tommy's shell and cheered as the turtle towed him around in an excited circle. "Whatever adventure we have, and wherever we go, I bet it'll be totally awesome!"

Coralie grinned and turned a somersault. "I think you mean *turtle-ly* awesome, Kai!" she said.

Kai gave her a friendly shove as Tommy shook with laughter and zoomed away. Kai felt happiness exploding through him. He was sure they were going to have another adventure very soon—and he couldn't wait!

Turn the page to learn more about the awesome Arctic and the creatures that live there!

THE ARCTIC

The Arctic Ocean is the most northern body of water on Earth. It is covered by ice all year round—meaning a large proportion of the ocean in the Arctic is dark.

At around 5.5 million square miles (8.9 million square km), the Arctic Ocean is the world's smallest ocean! It covers less than three percent of the surface of the Earth.

The temperature of the Arctic Ocean is consistently around 28°F (-2°C,) although the conditions above the water depend on the season. Winter lasts from September to May.

Several countries have territories that reach into the Arctic—Norway, Sweden, Finland, Iceland, Greenland, the United States, Canada, and Russia.

Around 4 million people live in the Arctic region. Many of these are indigenous groups that have lived there for millennia.

The Arctic consists of many dramatic landscapes, including sea ice, glaciers, mountains, rivers, coastal wetlands, and the ocean! There is a wide variety of wildlife, too. Some species that you'll find in the Arctic are walruses, whales, Pacific salmon, Arctic foxes, and polar bears.

ENVIRONMENTAL IMPACT

The Arctic is facing a number of threats, including oil and gas development, mining, and traffic from shipping and tourism. However, the biggest threat to the Arctic is climate change.

As temperatures rise, the ice melts. This could lead to an ice-free Arctic before the end of this century. While the effects of global warming are felt all over the Earth, it's predicted that warming in the Arctic is increasing at a rate of around two to three times faster than the rest of the world.

The decline in sea ice has a disastrous effect on the wildlife, too. Animals like polar bears need the sea ice in order to hunt for food.

Conservation groups around the world are looking at ways to reduce the impact of climate change in the Arctic and protect the animals and people who call it home.

We can help reduce climate change by saving energy and minimizing our carbon footprints. Small changes, such as walking or riding bikes, taking public transportation rather than driving, and turning off lights when we leave a room will help.

MEET TOMMY
THE TURTLE

Tommy is Kai's hawksbill sea turtle! Hawksbills get their name from their pointed beak. They can also be recognized by the distinct pattern of overlapping scales on their shells.

Hawksbills live in tropical oceans, predominantly in coral reefs. They eat sponges that they extract from crevices in the reef using their narrow beaks. They also eat sea jellies and sea anemones.

Not only does Tommy help Kai with his adventures, turtles are a fundamental link in marine ecosystems and help to maintain the health of coral reefs and seagrass beds.

Unfortunately, hawksbill turtles are critically endangered, mainly due to human impact. They are hunted for their shells and eggs. They can become caught in fishing nets and are affected by the reduction in coral reefs, making it harder for them to find the food they need to survive.

LEARN MORE ABOUT WONDERFUL WALRURES

Walruses are adapted to live in the Arctic. Males and females have large tusks—up to 3 feet (0.9 m) long—that they use to pull themselves onto sea ice. They also use their tusks to break breathing holes into the ice from below, fight other walruses, and defend themselves.

Walruses have other characteristics that help them survive in the Arctic. They have sensitive whiskers that help detect food on the dark ocean floor. Walruses' favorite foods include clams, molluscs, shrimp, and sea cucumbers.

Walruses have blubbery bodies that allow them to live comfortably in the low polar temperatures. The blubber can be up to 4 inches (10 cm) thick!

Climate change is the biggest threat that walruses face. With sea ice melting, walruses have to travel farther from their feeding grounds to rest. With less sea ice, walruses are also more likely to be disturbed by passing ships, which changes their behavior.

About the Author

Linda Chapman is the best-selling
author of more than 200 books. The
biggest compliment she can receive is
for a child to tell her he or she became
a reader after reading one of her books.
She lives in a cottage with a tower
in Leicestershire, England, with her
husband, three children, two dogs,
and one pony. When she's not writing,
Linda likes to ride, read, and visit
schools and libraries to talk to people
about writing.

About the Illustrator

Mirelle Ortega is a Mexican artist based in Southern California. She grew up in the south-east of Mexico, and developed a true love of magic, vibrant colors, and ghost stories. She also loves telling unique stories with interesting characters and a touch of magic realism.

JOIN NAYA AND HER FRIENDS FOR THEIR NEXT ADVENTURE IN...

MeRMaids ROCK

The Midnight Realm

by Linda Chapman

Illustrated by Mirelle Ortega

4

COMING SOON!